# CAMP KIDS

## AND

## THE RAINY DAY

Stone Fence Publishing

KEEP SWIMMING WITH THE CAMP KIDS IN MORE ADIRONDACK
ADVENTURES...

BOOK 1

CAMP KIDS AND THE UNDERWATER ADVENTURE

BOOK 2

CAMP KIDS AND SERPY'S WILD ADVENTURE

BOOK 3

CAMP KIDS AND THE TREASURE MAP


AND COMING SOON

BOOK 5

CAMP KIDS AND THE SEES ALL

# CAMP KIDS

## AND

## THE RAINY DAY

## WRITTEN & ILLUSTRATED

## BY SHARON SWAIN

Cover design by Sharon Swain

*Published by:*

Stone Fence Publishing

Burnt Hills, NY, 12027

USA

Printed in the United States of America

First printing 2013

ISBN: 978-0-9827847-3-0

www.stonefencepublishing.com

FOR HEIDI, KEVIN, AND DEBBIE

THANK YOU:

MARK, COLIN, SOPHIE, KAREN, KRISTIN, DEBBIE, DAMIAN, AND SUSAN

# CONTENTS

# CHARACTERS

**Name:** Grace Sophia Galley
**Jobs:** third grader, little sister to Cole
**Interests:** swimming, writing, tumbling
**Quote:** "I think I read about that."

**Name:** Colin (Cole) Mark Galley
**Jobs:** fifth grader, big brother to Grace
**Interests:** swimming, collecting soccer cards, video games
**Quote:** "Which way now?"

**Name:** Julia Anne Morgan
**Jobs:** third grader, aspiring yogi master
**Interests:** swimming, yoga, cooking
**Quote:** "Oooo, ahhh, ummm!"

**Name:** Jacob (Jake) Holden Leftwich, III
**Jobs:** fifth grader, quarterback
**Interests:** surfing, swimming, treasure hunting
**Quote:** "Watch out, I'm coming through!"

# CHAPTER 1

# SUMMER AGAIN

"Cole, wake up, we're almost there," Grace said, poking her brother on the shoulder.

"Huh, what?" Cole grunted, opening his eyes.

"Look out your window. We're almost there," Grace said again. "I wonder if Julia will be there yet. I can hardly stand it. I'm so excited!" Grace looked out her window at the pine trees passing by, her knees bouncing. The car was making the steady climb up the last paved road on the way to their camp in the Adirondacks. In just a minute the small circular lake would come into view.

Cole sat up and looked out his window. "I bet I see the lake first." He rubbed his eyes and slipped his feet into

his sandals. "Hey Dad, can Grace and I get out and run down the dirt road?"

"Yeah Dad, can we, please?" Grace begged. "Dougal can come too," she added, stroking the fluffy dog's head.

Mr. Galley laughed. "Get your shoes on so you're ready. Where do you want out; at your clubhouse like last year, or at the start of the dirt road?"

The kids looked at each other, "At the start of the dirt," they both replied.

The car rocked as it left the pavement. They could hear the crunch of the dirt and pebbles under the tires. The brakes gave a little squeak as the car stopped and Cole and Grace jumped out with their small tan dog. They took off running down the road toward their summer vacation at camp.

"Cole, look, Julia's car is at her camp. Come on, let's go say hi," Grace squealed.

"Definitely, I'm dying to know what it was like to swim in the Caribbean," Cole cheered, turning back and calling to their parents, who were slowly following behind them in the car, "Can we stop at Julia's?"

Mrs. Galley popped her head out the window. "Sure, but just to say hello. It's late and we still have to unpack." She put her head back in the window and Cole heard her whisper to his dad, "Good, that'll give us time to talk about how to tell them."

"Uh, thanks, we'll be at camp in a minute." Cole hesitated, wondering what she was talking about. Dougal jumped on his leg beckoning him to hurry up. He turned and saw Grace rounding the wall of firewood at the back

of Julia's camp. Cole ran to catch up. He darted around the end of the wall and ran right into Grace and Julia, who were already hugging and talking a mile a minute.

"Oh Cole, it's so great to see you. I couldn't believe it when you guys weren't here yet. I was so nervous. What took you so long?" Julia asked. She had been pacing up and down the dirt road since she had arrived two hours earlier. She hadn't even unpacked her new stuffed animals, or put up her new posters on her camp bedroom walls.

"Our dad had to speak at a conference today. We didn't leave until after 7:00," Grace explained. "It was *so* frustrating."

"Julia, you have to tell me all about the Caribbean," Cole said.

"Oh, it was so amazing. I helped a manatee," she chirped. "But let's wait until Jake gets here in the morning then we can all tell about what we did over the winter."

15

Since Julia lives in Boston, Jake in California, Cole and Grace in upstate New York, and their friends Harvey and Olivia had moved to Africa for the year, they hadn't seen each other or swam together since the end of August last year.

"Well hello," Julia's dad said, stepping out the back door of the camp. "I'm glad you two are here. Julia would've walked all the way to Route 12 to meet you if we'd let her."

Julia's mom peeked her head around Mr. Morgan's shoulder. "Well, if it isn't the swimming trio. I bet you kids can't wait to get into the lake together."

Grace and Cole smiled and gave Julia an uncertain look. Had she told her parents about the fairy stones they found at the beginning of last summer?

"She means because we all joined swim team this year," Julia explained quickly. Her mom didn't know that last summer, on the first day at camp, the four friends had learned that they were water sprites. With the magical fairy stones they had found, they were able to breathe underwater and swim through underwater river channels that led to more lakes and rivers. They could explore endlessly with no time passing above water. Last summer they had even gone far enough to see channels leading to the Atlantic Ocean. But they weren't supposed to tell anyone, not even their parents. Being a water sprite was an honor and with that honor came a responsibility to protect the Adirondack waters and water animals.

They found out that the magic of the stones will only last while they are young enough to have an uninhibited belief. And when the magic is gone, all memory of the sprite world will disappear. So even though each of the kids' mothers had been sprites when they were young, they couldn't even tell them because they don't remember being sprites. Jake hadn't seen his mom for the last ten years anyway, so he didn't have to worry about keeping the secret.

"Oh yeah, the swim team is great. We love swimming," Grace smiled.

"Why don't you come in for some hot cocoa and tell us about it?" Mrs. Morgan offered. "The mosquitoes are bad tonight."

"I have a great chili lime spice I got in Cancun. It's so yummy, you have to try it," Julia added.

Cole tried to smile, thinking of sour, spicy, and sweet together. "Uh, thanks, but our mom said we have to help unpack."

"Yeah, sorry we've got to go, but as soon as we get up tomorrow let's meet at the clubhouse. I've got the key right here." Grace said, pulling out a twine necklace with a small black leather pouch that held her fairy stone, a skeleton key, and half of a wooden moose head they had found in the car at the bottom of the lake.

Julia's eyes lit up. "I'm so excited. Hey Mom and Dad, can I walk them down to their camp? They don't even have a flashlight."

"Sure honey," Mr. Morgan said. "But come right back. I want to try some of that hot chocolate."

"So where are we going first?" Cole asked as soon as they stepped onto the dark path heading toward the Galley camp. "The Atlantic Ocean or Sprite Slide World?"

"I'm up for anything!" Julia sang.

Cole and Grace couldn't help but laugh. Julia had a tendency to panic and sometimes even freak out when she got scared, which was almost always.

"Listen, I've been taking yoga classes all year. I worked a lot with my mom on deep breathing and I worked at the aquarium with her too. I wasn't even scared when I helped an alligator," Julia stated. "You know the animals seem to really like me." Dougal yipped and she bent to pet him.

"Well that doesn't surprise me. I bet Chippy missed you over the winter," Grace said. Chippy was Julia's animal guide. Each of the water sprites had an animal etched in their fairy stone. All except for Grace. Her stone just had a pair of eyes. Jake had a catfish and Cole had a loon. The animals acted as guides in the sprite world.

"He didn't have to miss me. He showed up at my window a few days after I left camp. He slept for the whole next day." Julia's eyes grew huge. "Holy smokes! I put him in my bag so that he didn't have to walk all the way back to camp and I  forgot to get him out." She turned and started running back up the path. "I've gotta go. See you at the clubhouse tomorrow!"

Cole laughed. "Well, she hasn't changed. Chili lime hot chocolate, gross." Cole shook his head. "Oh, listen to this, when I was asking if we could go to Julia's, I heard Mom and Dad say something about telling us more bad news. Do you know what they're talking about?"

"No, do you?"

"No, but I hope they tell us now. I can't stand it when they have bad news. I just want to get it over with. Come on, Dougal. Let's go to camp."

# CHAPTER 2
# BAD NEWS

"Do you guys want some of my famous Cajun cranberry muffins?" Julia asked, spreading a napkin on the log table in the clubhouse. She had moved the waterproof journals, maps, and books aside to make room.

"No thanks, I can't really do spicy first thing in the morning," Cole said, wrinkling his nose. "Jeeze Julia, I'm about to sneeze. How much Cajun did you put in those?"

Grace spoke up, not giving Julia a chance to answer. "So, we have some bad news." She had hardly slept last night thinking about it. The bad news was actually kind of exciting. "We have to leave next week and we'll be gone until the end of July."

"What?!?!" Julia screamed. "But you can't. What if

Harvey and Olivia don't come back? I can't stay here with just Jake. He'll get us lost and make me surf the whole summer," she began breathing quickly. "What if we run into that creepo Pierre from last summer, or those crazy kids who seemed to know everything about Cole? You can't leave." She put her muffin down, stood up, and began pacing. "I don't think I know enough yoga for this." Deep breath, "What am I going to do?" Deep breath, "What if the black jellyfish comes back?" Deep breath. "What if Harvey and Olivia have to stay in Africa? Oh, I have to sit back down. Oooo, ahhh, ummm." She began chanting.

Grace and Cole looked at each other.

"Don't you want to know where we are going?" Grace quietly asked.

"Oooo, ahhh, ummm. Almost. Oooo, ahhh, ummm. Okay, just one more, Oooo, ahhh, ummm." She took another deep breath, opened her eyes and waited.

"Our dad has to go to Paris for a conference with

the International Oceanography Association," Grace said. "A project that he did about clean water with his students this year has gotten a lot of attention. They want him to present to a group of environmentalists."

Cole added, "And since we haven't visited our grandparents this year, we're going to go and see them first in England. And after the conference we're going to the south of France and then Spain for a week with my dad's friend." He was trying not to smile. It was bad news to leave camp, but it was so exciting to think about swimming in the Mediterranean Sea. There are loads of sunken ships and even sunken cities in the Mediterranean. And, if he wasn't here, he wouldn't have to worry about that guy Pierre.

Pierre had been his uncle Kevin's best friend when they were young. They had been water sprites too. At the end of last summer, Grace, Cole, and the other sprite friends had found a treasure map of Kevin's. It led them to a locker full of Dakotis coins, underwater money. Just before they lost the magic of their fairy stones, Pierre started stealing the money. And now, somehow, Pierre is a sprite again and he is looking for Kevin or at least he was at the end of last summer. He had even put up wanted signs with Kevin's picture, but since Cole looks so much like Kevin did when he was eleven, it felt like Pierre was looking for Cole.

"Okay, Julia, you can handle this." Julia found talking to herself to be very helpful. "Think of something good." She shut her eyes tight and held her breath. Then her eyes shot open and she shouted, "Did you say Paris? And Spain? Oh my gosh, you can get me the things I need to make that soufflé in my French cookbook from my nana." She smiled and patted herself on the back. "There, I knew I could do it. I just need to focus on the good things."

Just then, the door to the clubhouse flew open. "I'm here. Let the party start!" Jake shouted, running into the clubhouse and jumping on Cole's lap. He started rubbing Cole's head. "Did you miss me?"

"Yeah man, I missed you."

"And what about you, do you forgive me yet?" Jake

asked Grace. At the end of last summer, Jake and Grace had gotten into an argument about how to spend the money they had found. Jake had wanted an undersurf board, and Grace thought they should buy supplies for swimming in the bigger lakes and oceans and on the Sees All bundle. It was an interactive map that linked the four camp kids and their sprite friends Harvey and Olivia, so that they could see when and where the others were swimming. Grace won.

Grace just rolled her eyes. She had been so annoyed with Jake at the end of last summer and she thought about it all winter, but she decided she would just let it go. "Yeah, whatever. So how was your winter? How was swimming in the Pacific? It didn't look like you went very far on the Sees All."

"No, I couldn't breathe right, and I couldn't go deep without feeling loads of pressure just like when we tried to get to the Atlantic last year. But, I did get really good at surfing the underside of waves. I rocked the beach." Jake put his arms out and hopped on the table, just missing Julia's muffins, and pretended to ride it like it was a wave.

"Have you guys seen Harvey and Olivia on the map lately?" Grace asked.

"I haven't seen them in about a month and they were still in Africa," Cole sighed. "Come on. Let's go swimming and see if they left us a note in the car," he suggested, not waiting for an answer but standing up ready to leave. "If they're here, it's on to Sprite Slide World. If not, we're heading to the Atlantic!"

"Okay dude, calm down, we know you want to see Olivia but just calm down," Jake chided, standing up and rubbing Cole's head again. Jake loved teasing Cole. Then a big smile crept across his face. "We're going to have to find a way to breathe in the ocean pressure. Probably we'll even have to stop in a store to ask. I think the guy at the Surf's Down shop might know something and while we're there, I could just pick up that undersurf board I never got to get last summer," he said, giving Grace a sideways glance. "You did say you used your uncle's advice from that notebook and sold golf balls at the Dakotis Club, right? So we do have money, right?"

"Yeah, let's buy the boy his undersurf board and make him happy already," Cole said, turning and heading out the door.

"I'm so going to beat you to the car. I'm the captain of my swim team," Jake gloated.

"Yeah, so is Cole and so am I," Grace said to herself.

"And so am I," Julia added. "Come on, Chippy, let's go see Coolcat and Looney." Chippy sat arms crossed, next to Dougal, refusing to move. "I said I was sorry. I didn't mean to forget you. I was just so excited to see everyone. I'll give you some more muffin," Julia offered, but Chippy wrinkled his nose, sneezed, and turned his head away. "How about some pretzels?" she asked. Chippy's and

Dougal's eyes lit up and their noses went in the air, sniffing at the pretzels that Julia held up. "But you have to forgive me." Chippy nodded his head up and down, took the pretzels, gave one to Dougal and they headed out the door.

Just then there was a loud clap of thunder and the sky lit up. Chippy jumped back into Julia's arms. Grace looked up at the sky as the wind picked up. The girls began to run just as sheets of rain began pouring down.

# CHAPTER 3

# RAIN

"Is it ever going to stop raining? I swear we're not even going to get to swim before you have to leave," Jake yelled, shaking his hands above his head. "And I need my undersurf board!"

It had rained for five days straight and the forecast called for more rain tomorrow. And not just a little bit of summer rain, but pouring, storming rain. It was the kind of rain where you're not allowed to swim. The kids had begged and pleaded, but the answer continued to be "No." They had played cards and board games and walked to the store with umbrellas to buy candy. They had watched TV and gone into town to see a movie at the old movie theater, but they still had not gone swimming.

"I know, we only have two more days before we have to leave. This is ridiculous," Cole grunted, flopping down into the Adirondack chair in the clubhouse. "The news said it might stop today, but now it's freezing, so our mom won't let us swim anyway."

"I know, good thing my mom brought these," Julia said, removing her fluffy winter hat and mittens. "Come on you guys. Let's just make the most of it. Look, it's hardly even sprinkling now. We could play outside."

"Yeah, or we could go pick raspberries," Grace suggested.

"Then Mom could make raspberry jam." Cole began to smile and rubbed his hands together. "I love raspberry jam!"

"Sure, fine. There's nothing else to do anyway," Jake grumped. He hugged himself and shivered. He was wearing shorts, socks pulled up as far they could go, and layered T-shirts. "New York weather is crazy. At home it's sunny and warm every day. Maybe my grandpa has some winter clothes I could use."

"Let's all get warm clothes," Grace said, standing up and heading for the door. "Come on, Cole, you can finally use the walking stick that Grandma got you at the craft fair."

"And I can finally use the matching rain boots and fleece-lined coat that my nana got me in London." Julia smiled. "Oh, wait till you see them, Grace. They're so classic." She got up and followed the kids out the door.

*****

"Whoa, that's a bright yellow, Julia. What was that word?" Grace laughed. "Classic, yes, I guess you could say *that* yellow is classic. I don't know about the trim though. And where on earth did you find a matching outfit for Chippy?" Chippy was running behind Julia wearing bright yellow rain boots, a bright yellow raincoat, and a bright yellow rain hat all lined just like Julia's.

"Oh isn't he cute. They're from my doll. All of my dolls' clothes fit him." Then she whispered, "I even had him wear a dress for Christmas." Julia smiled. Chippy hung his head a little lower, shaking it from side to side.

Dougal sniffed Chippy's boots, whimpered, and covered his eyes with his paw.

"You've got to be kidding, Julia. The poor thing looks ridiculous!" Jake reached down and took off Chippy's hat.

"Hey, leave him alone!" Julia grabbed the hat from Jake and placed it back on Chippy's head.

"Whatever, but I'm telling you, he's not happy."

"Which path do we take?" Cole asked, ignoring the hat debate. "Is it the first one or the second off the paved road?"

"I don't know, Mom just said take *the* path." Grace replied. "She said it would bring us right to the raspberries."

"Well, I say let's take this one," Jake declared, turning and heading down the first path into the dense woods.

Cole and the girls followed right behind. As they walked, the trees grew closer together and it began to get dark very fast. They walked in silence in single file, following the narrow path deeper in the woods.

"I thought raspberries needed sunlight to grow," Julia said, pulling at a leaf stuck to her fur-lined wrist.

"I was thinking the same thing. I feel like we've been walking for ages," Grace said.

Jake stopped. "Hey, did you hear that?"

"What?" Cole asked, bumping into him.

"Shh, there it is again." There was a faint song of groans in the distance.

Dougal ears perked up and he threw his head in the air and howled.

"It sounds like a rooster," Cole thought aloud.

"What would a rooster be doing here?" Julia laughed nervously.

"Look, I think I see a clearing." Jake took off running toward the streams of sunlight struggling to sift through the clouds and trees up ahead.

"Finally. I'm starving!" Julia squealed, pushing at Grace's back. "Go, Grace, go."

"All right, but something doesn't seem right. Chippy does it seem right to you?" Grace asked, looking around. "Julia, where'd you put Chippy?"

"What do you mean, he's right . . . ," Julia turned back, but there was no Chippy. She turned to the left and to the right and backward again. She looked between her legs and in her pockets and with each turn her breathing got quicker. She was starting to hyperventilate. "Holy macaroni, he's gone!"

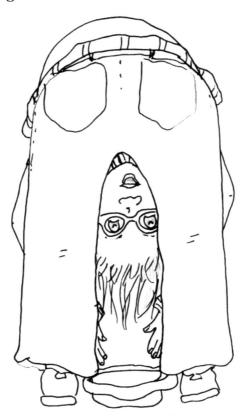

# CHAPTER 4
# THE BERRY PATCH

"It's that sound again. Did you hear it?" Grace asked, as the low song rumbled in the distance.

"Oh, that's probably just my stomach growling," Julia said between sobs. "I'm starving. Jake, if you didn't say you saw a clearing, my stomach wouldn't have thought it was getting raspberries, and it wouldn't be making this horrible noise. And Chippy wouldn't be missing," she added.

"Whoa, it's not my fault. Maybe Chippy got scared of your stomach and ran away," Jake countered.

"Yeah, you're right. Maybe Chippy knew I was hungry and went to get me food. Thanks, Jake, that's probably where he is."

"That is *so* not what I said. And stop worrying, he's a chipmunk, remember. He lives in the woods."

"Woof," Dougal added, wagging his tail.

"He's fine," Grace soothed, squeezing Julia's hand as the rumble sounded again even louder.

"Hey, I heard it that time," Cole said. "Jeeze, Julia, get control of your stomach."

"I can't help it. I can even smell raspberries now." She lifted her head and sniffed at the air. "Seriously you guys, I really can."

Dougal sniffed with Julia, whined and began pulling at his leash.

"Hey look, a real clearing this time." Jake bounded ahead again. "She's right," he called back. "I found the raspberry patch!"

"Finally, I won't starve!" Julia squealed.

The kids all rushed to join her and began picking the plump red berries from the small bushes that covered the clearing.

"Julia, slow down, you're going to make yourself sick," Jake called, watching Julia shove another handful of berries into her mouth.

"I know, but my stomach won't stop growling, can't you hear it? It's getting louder."

"Yeah, I don't think that's your stomach," Cole said, slowly turning toward the woods.

"Dude, I think you can stop eating. It's definitely not you," Jake said, looking into the woods with Cole as another low growl came even closer to the clearing.

"No, it's still my stomach. It has to be, because if it's not, then what is it?" Julia shrieked as the growl came again. She jumped onto Jake, grabbing his arm.

"I . . . think . . . it . . . might . . . be . . . a . . . bear," Grace stuttered, holding on to Cole.

Dougal yelped, and struggled against his leash, trying to head toward the sound.

"Well, what do we do?" Cole asked. He reached into his pocket and pulled out a slingshot. "I don't think this is going to help us fend off a bear."

"Hold on, let me think," Grace whispered, as the growl sounded again in the woods right in front of them.

Julia screamed and held on tighter to Jake. "Oh no, Chippy is loose out there somewhere!"

"Whatever we do, we can't panic," Cole whispered as the growling became even louder and even closer.

"It's right behind that tree, what are we supposed to do if we can't panic?" Jake asked through gritted teeth.

Just then an enormous black bear came ambling around the tree. Her head hung low and she was swinging her huge body back and forth. Dougal flopped in front of her, rolled to his back, and put all four fluffy legs straight up in the air. He looked up at the bear with giant sad eyes. The bear's growl sounded a lot more like a moan now that they could see her.

"Oh dear," Julia breathed, "I can do this. Just take a deep breath, and I can do this." She took a long deep breath, let go of Jake's hand, and walked toward the bear.

The other kids just stared. This couldn't be the same Julia who was terrified of nonexistent alligators and raccoon attacks.

"Okay Mrs. Beary, it's all right. We're going to help you," she said, walking right up next to the bear. "Are you hurt?"

The bear heard Julia's voice and stopped. She looked Julia right in the eye. No one moved. The bear's eyes were big and black, her nostrils were flared and she was breathing heavy. Julia didn't move, she just stared right back.

The bear dropped to her knees at Julia's feet and began moaning again. "Oh no, you guys, I think she's hurt."

"Uh, how do you know she's not going to maul us or something?" Cole asked, stepping closer to the bear. If

Julia wasn't afraid, he certainly wasn't going to be either.

"Yeah, how do you know?" Jake asked, coming in closer but still staying behind Cole.

"Hey, look," Grace said, pointing toward the sky. There was a bald eagle soaring right above them. It began circling right over their heads, getting lower and lower in the dark sky. She felt her fairy stone warming on her chest and she took it in her hand. "I think he's here to help us."

"I hope so, because I have no idea what we're supposed to do with a huge sobbing bear." Cole took a step closer, as Julia began to stroke the bear's head. "Julia, I thought you were scared of bears."

"I was, I mean I am. But this one needs us, something is wrong with her," Julia said as she began stroking the bear and moving around its big body.

"Um, isn't that when they get fierce?" Jake asked.

"You guys, the eagle. It's coming closer," Grace said, watching the sky as the eagle made slow perfect circles, each smaller and closer.

Just then a flash of yellow came running through the raspberry bushes. It was Chippy, chirping a mile a minute under his yellow hat. He climbed right up on the back of the bear and hugged her. Then he began jumping and squeaking even louder, making frantic motions with his hands and pointing at the bear and then back into the woods. Dougal jumped up to join the excitement.

"What? A baby? There's a baby in the woods?" Julia asked, desperately trying to understand.

Chippy pointed back to the bear, and rocked his

arms back and forth again. The bear began groaning and moaning again.

"Your baby is missing in the woods?" Cole asked, looking at the bear.

Chippy went wild jumping and pointing at Cole. The bear dropped her head and began moaning again.

"Well, what are we supposed to do about it?" Jake asked. "I don't know where baby bears hide."

"It's not hiding, it's in trouble. Right?" Grace asked.

Chippy quickly nodded his head up and down, knocking off the yellow rain hat and slyly kicking it toward Julia's bag.

"I see why," Julia said, holding up a chain. It was attached to a trap that was clamped on the mother bear's leg. Julia slowly followed the chain to the other end. It was attached to a tree behind the raspberry bushes. "Someone used the raspberries as bait to trap her. Her baby must have run off. Oh, Mrs. Bear, I'm so sorry."

"Listen, Jake and I will stay here and help free her. You two and Dougal follow Chippy and find the baby," Cole suggested, kneeling down to look closer at the trap.

"Yeah, and then just meet us back here," Jake added, heading over to the tree to examine the chain.

"Good idea, but take this," Grace said, rummaging through her bag and pulling out a walkie-talkie for the boys.

"Chippy wouldn't let us get lost, would you?" Julia asked. "Lead us to him, so we can help," Julia said, patting Chippy's head, then adding, "and please don't leave me like that ever again. I was so worried! But I guess I knew the whole time you must have had a good reason." Julia nodded her head, reassuring herself.

Chippy jumped up and took off following the trail farther into the woods. Julia, Grace, and Dougal followed, leaving the boys and mother bear behind.

# CHAPTER 5
# THE SEARCH

"Where are you taking us?" Julia screamed, trying to keep up with the chipmunk. The girls were able to catch glimpses of yellow darting over and under the broken branches and fallen trees. They had left the path and were now scrambling through the thick woods. Dougal was struggling to keep up as he yelped and jumped at every sound. His tail was now permanently tucked between his legs.

"We're going too far. How are we ever going to make our way back?" Grace worried. "And Dougal your supposed to protect us, not be scared," she said, bending to pet the dog. Dougal looked at her with sorry eyes and rubbed his head against her leg. "Oh it's all right." She patted his head. "We'll be fine."

"I don't know, it just keeps getting darker. Grace, I'm starting to get scared. Call the boys."

"Good idea." Grace turned on the walkie-talkie and pushed the button. *"Cole, come in, Cole."*

*"Chshk.. . . chshk. It's Cole here. We can't get the chain loose. We're using the walking stick to try to pry the trap open. Chshk . . . chshk. Over."*

*"It's Grace here. Chshk. Chippy keeps taking us deeper into the woods. I have no idea where we are. Chshk. Tell us when you get her free. Over. Chshk."*

*"Rightyo, will do. Chshk. Let us know when you find something. Chshk. Over and out."*

"Wait, did you hear that?" Julia stopped.

"Yeah, kind of like a cry, right?" Grace asked, just as a high pitched screech came from above. The girls looked up and saw the eagle dive down disappearing into the woods in front of them. Grace grabbed her fairy stone. It was warm again and shining. Could this be it? Could the eagle be her guide? She could hardly stand it, she wanted so badly to take it out of the pouch and look, but she was too afraid that she would lose it.

"Chippy, what is it?" Julia asked, stopping dead in her tracks. Chippy was running toward them but suddenly dropped to his belly and laid flat on the ground. Dougal immediately did the same and covered his eyes with his paws.

"Hide, quick," Julia screamed, diving to the ground.

"I don't think your yellow jacket is going to blend in very well," Grace whispered, joining Julia on the ground. She pulled some loose branches over Julia's back.

*"Chshk. Chshk. Come in, Walter."*

"Walter, who's Walter?" Grace whispered, turning the volume of the walkie-talkie lower.

*"Walter here. Chshk. Chshk. Do you have him? Over."*

"Yeah. Chshk. But he won't stop whining. Someone's gonna hear him."

The girls looked at each other as a loud whine could be heard over the walkie-talkie and somewhere in front of them at the same time.

"Well, shut him up! Knock him out or something. Chshk. I'll be there in min . . . Ahhh Stop it! Get off me!"

There was a loud shriek as the eagle dove from the sky toward the ground again.

"Get off me. Ahhh! Stop pecking me. Ahhh! I'm being attacked!"

The girls looked at each other again. They could hear the screams of the eagle and of the man, right behind them. They were hiding directly between the two men.

*****

"Who the heck was that? Did you hear that, Jake?" Cole grunted, while he leaned with all of his weight onto the walking stick.

"Yeah," Jake answered as he jumped up and hung from the stick, making the trap open a little bit. "We've got to hurry. Push!"

*****

"Who's he gonna knock out?" Julia asked through chattering teeth.

"Shh, he's coming," Grace whispered.

The girls ducked their heads and tried to quietly sink deeper in the leaves as the sound of footsteps got closer and closer. The crunch of the leaves landed right behind them.

"Well, well, well, what do we have here?" They heard the man say as he kicked at them.

Grace looked up at the tall man. He had a thick black mustache and small beady eyes in a head that was too small for his large frame. "Uh, hello, sir. We were just out berry picking and got a little lost." Grace pushed the

button on the walkie-talkie, hoping that Cole would hear and know what to do. "But, we know where we are now. So, we'll just be going." Grace rose to her feet and kicked at Julia's arm, and prayed that Chippy was hiding in her pocket or something. The last thing they needed was to explain why they had a chipmunk with them that was wearing a yellow rain outfit. Dougal peeked through

Grace's legs and began a low throaty, stuttered growl.

Julia stood and clutched Grace's arm so hard that she almost pulled her down. Her eyes had nearly popped out of their sockets and her mouth was pulled back making her look like someone pushed PAUSE at the moment between when she was deciding whether to scream or cry.

"Well now. I don't know if I should let a pair of little girls wander through the woods on their own." The creepy man said through his wiry mustache and smoke-stained teeth.

Grace checked to be sure the walkie-talkie button was still pushed in. "Uh, we're not alone. Nope, my older brother is just over there with our friend. He was just trying to get better reception on the phone to call our mom. He'll be right back." Dougal growled again. "And we have our dog."

*"Walter, come in Walter. Chshk. Is everything all right?"* The walkie-talkie was somewhere behind them.

"Darn thing. I must have dropped it when that bird attacked me.  Well, I guess you're in luck, ladies. I've got to find that, so I don't have time to worry about the two of you and your mop of a dog." The man turned, kicked Dougal and growled at him. Dougal yelped and hid behind Grace. The man laughed. "That ain't no dog." He turned and tromped back through the woods, still laughing.

*"Walter, come in. Chshk. This bear is going crazy. I can't hit it over the head, because it won't stay still. And the boss man called, he said . . . chshk . . . something about we gotta find a baby moose now too. Chshk."*

The man must have found the walkie-talkie.

*"Oh, keep quiet, Fred. I told you not to mention any of the animals on the walkie-talkie! If he calls back, find out if he needs a bald eagle. Chshk. Over."*

*****

55

"Help me, Cole. Pull!" Jake shouted.

"I am pulling! Hurry, the girls are in trouble. We have to hurry."

"On the count of three use all of your strength. I think we almost have it."

The boys were practically sitting on the walking stick, which was wedged in between the jaws of the trap. The bear was still moaning, but had stopped swaying and was trying to stay still, watching the trap, and waiting until it opened enough to pull her leg out.

"All right, Mrs. Bear, we need your help," Cole said softly. "Can you help push this with your leg maybe? I just don't think we're strong enough."

The bear lifted her back leg and even though the boys could see the trap ripping deeper into her flesh and pulling a claw away from the skin, she leaned even more and wrapped her toes around the bar. She pushed down with the kids, and the jaws opened another inch, just enough for the bear to pull out her paw leaving one claw behind.

"Great job," Jake cheered, patting the bear as she slowly tried to stand.

"We've got to bandage it somehow. Jake, look for something while I try to radio the girls."

"NO, DON'T!" Jake screamed, yanking the walkie-talkie from Cole's hand. "It might not be safe yet."

"Well, we can't just sit here and wait. He could have hurt them."

The bear nudged Cole and took a tentative step. She winced, but stepped again, and then she began hobbling through the woods, following the path the girls had taken. Cole followed right behind. Jake bent down and picked up the bear claw. He wiped it clean and put it in his fairy stone pouch.

57

# CHAPTER 6
# EAGLE EYES

"Julia, come on, we've got to get out of here," Grace pleaded, turning back to Julia.

"We can't," Julia stated, digging her heals into the dirt.

"Why on earth not?" Grace asked. "You don't want to see those guys again, do you?"

"No. The baby bear. If they take the bear, they'll be back for a moose and an eagle, and who knows what else. Grace, they are bad men. We have to stop them."

"I know, but, Julia, we can't do it alone, we have to go call the police or something." Grace tried to sound determined, but she knew they had to help now. Her fairy stone was warm on her chest again almost like it was helping to persuade her to stay. She looked up and the eagle was soaring right above them again. "What about the boys?"

"Well, radio them or something."

"I can't, what if the men hear?" Grace asked, watching as the eagle swooped, flew back toward her and swooped again into the woods behind her. It was making circles that were getting smaller and smaller in the dark sky. It was beautiful. She closed her eyes and she could imagine what the bird was seeing. The

tops of the trees, an occasional clearing, and . . . what? Was that a bear? And Cole and Jake? Grace opened her eyes and looked back to the sky. The eagle was swooping down into the woods behind. She closed her eyes and again and saw the trees and a glimpse of the bear bounding through the trees, with Cole and Jake trying to keep up. She saw the bear stop and wait for a second and then carry on lumbering through the woods. Then she saw herself, standing with her eyes closed, next to Julia. The boys were getting closer.

Grace opened her eyes. "Um, Julia, I think the boys will be here any second." She closed her eyes again. She saw them just a few hundred yards away. She opened her eyes and watched as the eagle's swooping circle got smaller and smaller as the boys got closer.

"Are you all right?" Julia asked. "Do you have a headache or something?"

The eagle was now circling directly above them. "Right there," she said, pointing to the woods.

Julia looked just as the bear bounded over a rock and landed at her feet. The boys came over the rock a second later.

"Thank you, thank you, thank you. You're all right," Cole panted, falling into Grace to hug her. "I was so scared that creepo took you guys." He hugged her again, and then hugged Julia. He bent down and hugged Dougal. "I'm so sorry buddy. We'll get those guys. I promise." Dougal wagged his tail and licked Cole's nose.

"Yeah, we're happy you're okay," Jake added, punching Grace in the arm and giving Julia a half smile. He looked very uncomfortable.

Julia dove into Jake and hugged him, "We were so worried about you too!"

"Okay," he said, pushing her off, "that will do."

"Oh my, are you all right?" Julia asked, looking at

the bear. Chippy had already inspected the wound and was digging through Julia's bag. He poked his head out and lifted up a silk scarf. Julia slowly took the scarf, "Yeah, okay. My grandma did get this for me in India, but it is kind of ugly. Why would anyone want golden stripes? It can just clash so easily with your jewelry."

Chippy ran off into the woods and returned with some bark from a birch tree. He rubbed it on the wound. He pulled off his yellow rain jacket and pushed it into the bag, took the scarf from Julia and wrapped up the wound, kicking off his boots as he worked.

"Great job, Chippy, and I guess you're right, we should lose the yellow." Julia took off her jacket and neatly folded it before putting it in her bag. "Good thing it's not raining anymore."

The bear licked Chippy's head and began moaning. She started swaying and nodding her head up and down and side to side.

"So what now?" Cole asked. "Which direction did they go?"

"Hold on," Grace said, looking up to the sky. The eagle was nowhere to be seen, but she closed her eyes anyway. Immediately, she was up in the sky again, looking down into a clearing at a broken down hunting cabin. There was a fenced-in part on the side. The baby bear was lying on the ground, and the man, Walter, was standing above it.

The other man, Fred, was on the other side of the bear with his eyes shut and a log held above his head. His legs were trembling. Grace could hear Walter yelling at Fred to just do it, when the eagle must have swooped down because all of a sudden Grace was diving between the men. The eagle knocked Fred over and made him drop the log. Then it soared up again toward the sky, turned and dove, this time at Walter, heading straight for his face and pecking at him. The eagle flew back up into the sky.

Grace could see the trees below and then she could see herself standing on the ground with the bear and the other camp kids. They were all looking at her like she was having a fit or something. She opened her eyes.

"Don't worry, I'm all right. I'll explain it all to you later. We have to hurry. This way." Grace took off toward the cabin, stopping to close her eyes and using the eagle to guide her.

They ran through the woods until they got close enough to peek between the trees and see the cabin, the men, and the baby bear. Walter was still trying to convince Fred to hit the bear. The baby bear was just lying still with his paws over his head.

"Look, the latch on the fence is just a piece of wood," Jake said.

Chippy bounced up and down on Julia's yellow boot. He climbed up her leg, sat on her shoulder, and

began chattering in her ear. "Okay, okay," she said. "I think Chippy wants to do the latch."

"Perfect," Grace said as she pulled her journal from her bag. She drew a quick diagram of the scene and charted out the plan of action. She quickly told the group their part of the plan.

*****

The first few parts of the plan went without a hitch. Chippy unlatched the gate and he and Julia headed safely off into the woods. The eagle swooped into the cage, as the mother bear called her baby, and the baby bear looked up and called back, but it was too scared to move. The boys were quickly going through their slingshot ammunition as the eagle continued to swoop, but the baby still wouldn't move.

Grace couldn't stand it anymore. She stood up and headed straight toward the cage. She was going to get that baby no matter what. Dougal tugged at her pant leg, trying to stop her, but she kept walking, pulling him along the ground behind her.

"Grace! NO!" Cole shouted.

"I have to. We can't do this for much longer!" She marched farther into the opening still dragging Dougal.

"Hey, leave me alone," Fred yelled at the eagle.

"The animals have gone mad!" Walter screamed.

Grace was a foot from the gate when the eagle dove toward her, stopping her and Dougal in their tracks. The mother bear pushed past her and bounded through the gate. She stood on her hind legs and growled so loudly that the two men, who were facing the other direction, stood straight and put their hands in the air, like they were being arrested.

The mother bear pushed them both aside with her massive paws and hobbled toward the baby. She nudged it forward and the baby scampered through the gate and off into the woods. The mother stood on her hind legs and growled again. Walter and Fred, who had turned to  watch, cowered under their arms.

"You can have your baby back," Fred squealed.

"But we need the money," Walter shouted.

The bear growled again and landed on her forepaws right in front of Walter.

"Yeah, yeah, okay you can have your baby," he whispered, stepping back and tripping over Dougal who had followed the bear into the cage. "Watch out!" he grumbled, landing on his bottom, with his hands still in the air. "We'll just find ourselves a moose or eagle to get the money, or maybe we'll just take your little mop," he laughed.

Dougal growled and began running in circles around the two men, using his leash like a rope.

The eagle swooped down and gave one last shriek and peck at the top of his head before heading back into the ever darkening sky. Grace quickly unclipped Dougal, tied a knot in the leash, and they ran into the woods.

# CHAPTER 7
# MORE BAD GUYS

"I can't believe they caught them," Julia said, leaning back in her chair at the clubhouse as the rain pelted the tin roof.

"I can't believe we didn't get in trouble for being so far out in the woods," Cole said.

"I know. My grandparents bought our story."

"Well we didn't really lie. We did go berry picking and we did find the bear in the trap and you guys did let him free. I guess that it's not so unbelievable that we could get lost," Grace said.

"Yeah, I was thinking the same thing. But the important thing is they *did* believe us and those meanies have been stopped. I hope the bears are all right," Julia sighed, hugging Chippy a little tighter.

"Yeah, I thought for sure those dumbos would be gone by the time the police got there," Jake added. "Boy, were they a pair of dodoes."

"That was a great idea to tie them up Dougal. I bet that really slowed them down," Grace said, patting the dog's head. "I bet they were still looking for this," she said, holding up a small notebook. "I can't believe you and Chippy found it. Walter must have dropped it when the eagle swooped down at him and he lost his walkie-talkie. Oh, that reminds me," Grace added quietly. She stood and wandered over toward the fireplace.

"What?" Julia asked.

"I was just wondering," she whispered, taking her fairy stone out of its pouch. She couldn't believe that she hadn't checked it yet. There must be a picture of an eagle now. She took a deep breath and looked at the stone, but there was still just a pair of eyes. No eagle.

70

Julia walked over behind Grace. She looked at the stone. "Oh, Grace, I'm so sorry. You were hoping that the eagle was your guide, right?"

"What happened with the eagle anyway?" Cole asked. "How did you know what he was doing?"

"Well, when I closed my eyes, I could see everything that he could see. And my stone felt warm every time he was near. I thought for sure he was my guide."

"Well, sounds like he was. Maybe your stone is just broken or something," Jake said.

"How could it be broken?" Grace snapped. "It can't be broken because I don't know how to fix it." She held her stone, hung her head, and closed her eyes. She tried to see like the eagle. She tried to get some sort of sign, but it just wouldn't work. She was going to have to face it: she still didn't have an animal guide. Grace sighed and opened the notebook. "Let's take a look at this."

The kids gathered around and read over Grace's shoulders as she slowly flipped through the pages. There were phone numbers and a few names, and there were lists and lists of animals. Some of them were checked off, and some were highlighted, including the black bear.

"What do you think it means?" Julia asked.

"Dudette, open your eyes. It's right there. They were capturing these animals and giving them to, I don't know, one of these guys listed up here," Jake said, flipping to the front of the book.

"We should've given this to the police," Cole said.

"Yeah, but it's a bit late now, we can't really say we just found it, or that we forgot about it," Grace said, taking a deep breath. "We're going to have to try to do something about it ourselves."

"What?!? These men are criminals. We can't do anything." Julia shivered, hugging Chippy even tighter.

"Well, if we're going to do anything about this, we'd better hurry. Look at the deadline dates on the Adirondack animals," Cole said, pointing to the list. "Moose: July 4, great blue heron: July 4, white-tailed deer: July 4, loon: July 4, chipmunk: July 4, bald eagle: July 4. You guys, that's in two days."

"Yeah, and don't forget, that's also the day we leave," Grace added.

"Oh no, I forgot about that. Well, I didn't exactly forget, I tried hard not to remember," Julia whined.

"Well, what do we do?" Jake asked.

"We go to the library. We need to use the Internet," Grace stated.

# CHAPTER 8
# THE LIBRARY

"Oh my gosh, these names keep getting hits on Most Wanted lists. And not just from here, from all around the world," Grace said, looking up from the computer.

"Shh. The last thing we need is someone finding out what we're doing. The librarian is looking at us," Cole whispered.

"Did you say Most Wanted lists?" Julia choked out, shaking her head back and forth. "Oh no, no. We're getting in too deep."

"Just calm down. There's nothing illegal about looking up names on the computer," Jake said, shifting in his seat to get a better look. "I think I've seen that guy before. What does it say he's wanted for?"

"Um, let's see. This one is from Spain. Look right there; wanted for animal trafficking." Grace clicked the mouse. "And here." She pointed to the computer. "This is from Brazil and I don't read Portuguese, but it looks like animal trafficking again." She clicked the mouse. "And this one is some sort of international animal rights group and these names come up as one and two on their most dangerous list. Look there are even pictures. You guys, I think Julia might be right. We might be in over our heads." Grace looked at the boys, took a deep breath, and twisted her braids around her fingers.

"Is everything all right over there, kids?" Mrs. Pillawickee, the librarian, asked in her grandmotherly voice.

"Uh, yes, ma'am. We were just wondering, um, if we could use the printer." Jake smiled his best old-lady-pleasing smile, showing his perfect white teeth and fluttering his eyelashes, right at the librarian.

"Oh, okay dear, just hit print and you can collect it over this way." Mrs. Pillawickee took Jake's elbow and led him toward the back corner. "It's so nice when you boys use manners these days."

Jake smiled back at the kids and took the paper as it drifted off the printer. He quickly folded it. "Thank you so much, ma'am," he drawled, looking up through his eyelashes at the librarian and giving a little bow.

"Any time dear, that's what we're here for." She smiled again at Jake and went to take his hands as he hurried to push the paper behind his back. But he had it folded the wrong way. "Is that Spike, dear?"

Grace stepped closer. "Spike? Who is Spike?" she asked.

"No, that wouldn't be Spike now would it?" Mrs. Pillawickee shook her head. "This memory of mine doesn't always work so well. Spike would have left nearly thirty years ago now. What a nice boy he was. Mean father though. I always thought that was why he left without a word.

"Can you imagine a twelve-year-old boy just up and leaving town? Just like that." She shook her head again snapping out of her memory. "Oh, yes, you wanted to print. Right this way, my dear."

"Um, we already did," Cole said.

"Yes, that's right. You wanted a photo of Spike. Maybe I have one here." She turned her head toward the desk and the children all looked at each other and shrugged their shoulders. They followed her to the desk, where she proceeded to pull out piles of photographs. "Now, I've kept photos of all my helpers. If I remember correctly, Spike was interested in animals. Yes, that's right, he was very interested in endangered species right before he left. Well, if I look I think I might still have the book he was reading when he left. He left it right here on the desk with a note to me. Can you imagine, just twelve years old."

The librarian began sifting through some books on a low shelf. Grace picked up the photos and began sifting through them. "Is it all right if I keep looking at the pictures?"

"Oh, yes dear, see if you can find Spike while I just find this book." She bent again toward the low shelf, humming, and picked out a book. "Oh my, I haven't seen this in such a long time. I knew a boy once who spent hours with this book. What

78

was his name? Now give me a minute and I'll remember. Spud? Point? Spear? Oh, my memory is not what it used to be."

The kids all looked at each other again.

"Was it Spike?" Julia asked.

"Oh my, well yes, I think it was, dear. Yes, what a nice boy he was. Such a shame when he left. I always thought it was because of his dad and the hunting." She looked up. "How do you know Spike? Are you Native American as well, dear?"

"Um, no, I was just um . . ." Julia looked at her friends again, not knowing what to say.

Grace held up a picture. "Is this Spike?" It was a picture of a boy with dark skin and long, straight dark hair. He was looking at the camera, and his dark eyes looked as though they were looking straight through you.

Jake stepped back from the picture looking very uncomfortable and mumbled under his breath, "Yeah, I'm

sure I've seen him before."

"Oh yes, that's Spike. What a sweet boy. Shame when he left." She shook her head and looked up at the children again. "Oh dear, here I am talking and you wanted to use the printer. It's right this way." She began walking toward the printer.

"Uh, can we just check out this book instead,

please?" Grace asked, holding up the endangered species book. "And would it be all right if I borrowed this picture?"

"He was such a sweet boy. Oh, and look at that bear claw. He told me that he saved that bear from his father." She wrote down the information in the check-out log and handed Grace the book. "Now you kids be sure to come back and visit, especially you, sweetheart," she added, winking at Jake.

Jake smiled his sweetest smile again. "Yes, ma'am. I always come straight to you when I need information." He bowed and walked backward out the door.

# CHAPTER 9
# LINNY

"Now what?" Cole asked, back at the clubhouse. "Even if this guy Spike looks just like the guy on the Most Wanted list, it couldn't be him. He was all about saving the animals when he was a kid."

"I know, it just doesn't make sense. Why would he be paying creepos like that Walter and Fred to capture animals when he wants to protect animals?" Julia asked.

"Dude, I don't know, but I'm totally putting this bear claw on my necklace too," Jake said, taking the bear claw out of his pocket.

"What do you mean on your necklace *too*?" Grace asked.

Jake pointed to the picture of Spike that was on the

wooden table in front of the kids. "Right there, next to his fairy stone pouch. Holy smokes. He has a fairy stone pouch! I didn't even see that before."

"Oh my gosh, you're right. And didn't she say that he disappeared about thirty years ago? When he was twelve?" Grace asked.

"And if our moms are thirty-nine, wouldn't that make them nine and water sprites at the same time? They were younger, but if they were all water sprites they might have met him, or at least heard about him before." Julia thought out loud.

"Well, that would make my mom twelve. She's forty-two now. Wherever she is," Jake grumbled.

"Come on, let's go ask. Somebody is bound to know something." Cole stood and headed toward the door. The rain was teaming down on the tin roof again. Rivers of water were falling in front of the door.

*****

"Spike, you said?" Jake's grandpa asked. "Yeah, your mom knew Spike. I was happy to see the back of him, I can tell you that."

"Now he was only a boy, Stephen," Jake's grandma said. "Linny was just precocious at that age. And all they were doing was trying to stop his dad from trapping those poor animals."

The kids all looked at each other and then at Jake. He had hung his head and was shaking it back and forth.

"Are you saying that my mom was friends with this guy?" Jake's face was turning red and he was visibly starting to shake.

"What is it, darling? Why are you asking about Spike anyway? He hasn't turned up again has he?" Jake's grandma asked.

"Oh, we just read the name on the wall at the clubhouse. We were just wondering who he was," Grace quickly replied.

"Yes, Linny and Spike were always writing in journals. You know I always thought she knew something about where he went. They were so close and Linny wasn't even upset when he left." Jake's grandma stood up and walked toward the kitchen. "How does some fresh homemade granola sound?"

"No thanks, Grandma," Jake said with a renewed look of determination. "Hey, Grandma, do you still have any of those books? You know the ones that my mom wrote in?"

"Well now, I don't know. Stephen, where did you put that box of Linny's?"

"Oh that. It's still in her room; under your bed, Jake." Jake's grandpa took a deep breath and quietly added, "I just didn't have the heart to move it."

Jake turned and headed straight for the bedroom. Cole and Julia followed.

"Um, excuse me, Mrs. Shand, but do you think Jake's mom ever heard from Spike again?" Grace asked.

"Well, now that you mention it, she did say something about him. You know, it was right before she left. Stephen, do you remember? What was it that she said?"

"She read about him in the newspaper. It was right before she applied for that blasted job that took her away from us." Jake's grandpa picked up the TV remote and turned it on, taking himself out of the conversation.

"You'll have to excuse him, dear, he still has a hard time talking about Linny leaving. We'll just never understand how our little girl could just up and leave like that, especially with Jake being just a baby."

"I'm sorry, I shouldn't have asked. I'll just go and see if Jake found the box. Thanks." Grace turned and hurried into the bedroom.

*****

"I can't believe this has been here the whole time. Look, it's got everything." Jake pulled notebooks and journals, letters and diaries out of the box that he found under his bed. "I mean I always saw it under there, but I just assumed it was full of towels or my grandpa's old clothes or something."

"Jake, there's, like everything your mom ever thought in here," Julia said, opening a diary marked Summer 1979.

"Yeah, and look at this." Cole held up a fairy stone pouch. It was empty. The kids already knew that her retired stone was in the clubhouse. But hanging from the pouch was a bear claw, just like the one Spike was wearing in the picture.

"You've got to be kidding me." Jake grabbed the pouch. "This just keeps getting better, doesn't it? What if we find out my mom still has something to do with this guy?"

Jake hung his head again and covered his face with his hands.

"Jake, your grandma said they were just trying to save the animals. Your mom was good. I'm sure that she had a really good reason to leave. It must have been incredibly important to leave you." Grace reached out to touch Jake's shoulder, but he pulled away.

"Yeah, Jake, my mom always tells me how all the younger kids wanted to grow up to be just like her," Julia said, sitting down on the bed next to Jake. "And how she even saved a bear one time. I was just thinking about that. Now you've saved a bear just like her."

Jake snapped his head up. "I'm not just like her. I wouldn't ever leave my baby."

"You might if you thought you had to," Cole said, handing Jake a piece of paper that he had pulled from the box. "Sorry, I didn't mean to read it first."

Jake took the paper. It was a letter from his mom. There was no date, but there was a picture of his mom holding him as a baby and hugging and kissing him. He was laughing. Jake stared at the picture and tears started to slowly escape from the corners of his eyes.

"My dad never talks about her. I've never even seen a picture of me with her. How could this picture have been here for ten years and I never knew about it?" Jake wiped his eyes and looked at the letter. He read it quietly.

*Dearest Jake,*

*I love you more than you could ever know. It is killing me to leave you, but I know that your father and grandma and grandpa will take good care of you until I get back. I've just found out some terrible things are happening and my new job is giving me a chance to make some things right in the world, the world that you are going to grow up in. I hope that you never read this, and that I make it back before you even have a chance to miss me. But, always remember that I love you and that making the decision to leave you was the hardest decision I have ever had to make. And please know that I made it for you. I love you always.*

*Mom xoxox*

Jake looked up at his friends. He held the letter out to the girls and began looking through the box again. He was frantically pulling out papers and pictures and newspaper articles.

"What are you looking for?" Cole asked. "I can help."

Jake frantically pulled things from the box.

Cole grabbed him. "Jake, are you okay?"

Jake stopped and looked at Cole and the girls who had now finished reading the letter. "I always knew that she loved me. And I always knew that she must have had a good reason to leave, but . . ." he sniffed, "no one ever helped me believe it. You know? My dad never says anything, I mean like *never* says anything about my mom. And my grandma and grandpa just act like it never happened. They just talk about when she was young, never about her leaving, even when I ask. And now I have proof. I just know that she is doing something amazing and that she's still planning to come back. I bet you anything, if I look through this box, I'm going to find out where she is and what she is trying to do." Jake started plowing through the papers again and quietly added, "And then I can go and help her."

"Is it all right if we help?" Grace asked.

"Yeah, Jake, I really want to help you find your mom," Julia said, putting her arm around him again. He didn't even pull away this time. "I always knew that she loved you. Your mom is amazing to sacrifice so much."

"Yeah, dude, let us help. If we work together, we can do anything." Cole put his hand out. "What do you say?"

Grace and Julia added their hands to the pile and waited for Jake. He slid his hand underneath and smiled. "Yeah, I think we make a pretty good team. Okay, one, two, three . . ."

"WATER SPRITES!"

# CHAPTER 10

## CLUES

By the time they finished sifting through the box, it was getting dark. They had spent the last five hours in Jake's bedroom, refusing offers of unsweetened prunes and eggplant protein shakes. Thankfully, Julia managed to sneak in some ice-cream bars when she ran back to her camp for a sweatshirt.

"Well, I'm exhausted. I can't believe that it's the same day that we helped the bear and caught those guys," Cole said, raising his arms up to stretch as he stood up from the floor.

"I know. At least we can't say we were bored today," Grace said, standing to join Cole, shaking out her sleeping feet.

"Jake, I'm so happy for you. Your mom is great!" Julia sighed. "Everything she wrote about was amazing. She and that guy Spike must have saved at least a hundred animals by the time they were our age."

"Thanks, Julia," Jake sighed. "But I still have no idea how to find her."

"The only other place I can think to look is the library. Your grandpa mentioned that your mom read about Spike in the newspaper right before she took that job," Grace thought out loud.

"What do you mean my grandpa mentioned it? When?" Jake scowled at Grace.

"Well, um, I talked to him and your grandma quickly when you went into your bedroom to find the boxes."

"Why didn't you say anything? Grace, you always have to know more, don't you?" Jake walked over to a dresser. "I knew I'd seen that guy before." He opened the top drawer and pulled out the newspaper liner from under his clothes. All of the kids looked down and staring back at them was a photograph of Spike. The newspaper that was being used as a drawer liner was dated May 2001. "I knew I had seen that guy before. I just knew it."

"I'm sorry I didn't say anything Jake. I didn't know." Grace hung her head. She was desperate to read the paper but knew she had to give Jake time.

"Yeah, yeah, me too. Just when you mentioned the newspaper, I knew it would be this." Jake picked up the paper. "Oh here, Grace, you read it."

The article talked about how Spike had been working for an international charity for years. He was working to save animals that were in danger throughout the world because of damage humans were causing, like oil spills and overfishing. Then it said something about a ten-million-dollar donation given for a new research fund and that Spike was in charge.

"Your mom must have gotten a job with Spike," Cole looked up at Jake, "and if we can find out which charity it was, we can find Spike."

"My dad comes tonight. I will try to get his computer and see if I can find out anything," Julia stated, standing up.

"Do you want me to reread anything tonight to see if I can see anything different?" Grace asked, hesitating slightly. She didn't know if Jake was mad at her or not anymore.

"Yeah sure, whatever. Here, take her diaries. You know more about that girly stuff than I do anyway."

"Well, I'm going to check out Spike's endangered animals book we got from the library. If we can find out what made Spike leave, that might help too," Cole said, pulling at Grace's arm. "We'd better go."

Julia walked toward the door but stopped and hugged Jake first. "I'm so happy for you!"

Jake pushed her off. "Yeah, yeah, all right Dudette, no need for that. I'll see you in the morning," Jake said continuing to push Julia out the door with a smile spreading across his face. His mom didn't just leave him.

# CHAPTER 11
# THE BOATHOUSE

"Right, the only information I found was that the charity was Dutch and that it went bust in a massive scandal. The ten million dollars were stolen in August 2001," Julia said, raising her eyebrows, and digging her toes into the sand on the beach. "It doesn't sound like a coincidence does it?"

"My mom left in August of that year. She must have known something about it," Jake sighed.

"Well, I found something," Cole offered, opening the library book. "Check this out. The note Spike left Mrs. Pillawickee is right here, and it tells her that he was going to Amsterdam; the one in Holland not here in New York, to help a charity specializing in marine mammals."

"Oh my gosh," Grace blurted, fumbling through the pages of one of Linny's diaries. "In your mom's diary from when she was twelve, she wrote all about how badly she wanted to leave with Spike so she could help the animals too. I even think these weird cave painting things are notes from Spike. Look, they've all been folded like they were mailed. And the same images keep repeating at the end every time. I can't figure it out though." Grace handed the pages to Jake.

"Let me see, I'm great at those things," Julia offered. "My dad taught me all about ciphers when I was a little kid. I think he was trying to distract me because I was scared to fly and I kind of freaked out sometimes. That was before I got so good at my deep breathing," Julia smiled. "But anyway, I'm really good at them. They're like puzzles." She took the pages from Jake.

"Well, all I know is that I need to swim. It's finally not raining." Cole looked up, squinting at the sky. "Thank you, sunshine! Our mom said we can swim all day."

"Oh my gosh, you guys, it's so easy." Julia looked up smiling. "The folds are part of the puzzles. Look, you just fan fold and then fold these in." Julia folded the paper, connecting the tops and bottoms of each line. "They must have still been sprites. Look here. At the end it says "Let's meet" and then a number. We just have to figure out where they met."

"I know," Grace shrieked. "It's right here in this diary. Jake's mom drew a map. Here, it looks like Chase's Lake." Grace lifted the diary for the others to see.

"Well, let's go. We're not going to find out standing here, are we?" Jake asked. He ran into the water and disappeared under the surface with the waiting Coolcat and Looney.

Cole and Grace shoved the books into Grace's Bounteous Bag (the waterproof, bottomless bag she bought last summer) and they followed Julia into the lake.

The kids swam through the channel connecting their small lake to Brantingham Lake, and then on to Catspaw Lake and finally through the channel leading to Chase's Lake. They immediately found the meeting place. It was an old, unused boathouse. They swam under the broken lakeside boat door and climbed up a ladder and out of the water. They were now inside the boathouse without anyone seeing them.

"This place is awesome," Julia said. "Look at those posters." They were of all sorts of water animals, like walruses, manatees, and river otters.

"And check out all of these notes. They're in the same code," Grace said. "Julia, you'll have to teach us how to read them."

"Yeah but, we need to focus on finding something that will lead me to my mom." Jake reminded them, climbing a ladder into the rafters where a landing had been made.

"Hey, what's up there?" Cole wondered, starting up the ladder behind Jake.

"Dude, it looks like someone has been living here. And I mean like, recently." Jake's voice was muffled as he disappeared onto the landing.

"Yeah, there's tea over here and it's still warm," Julia's voice cracked. "We need to get out of here." She tried to take a deep breath, but it got caught in her throat as she turned and looked out of the dirty, oil-smudged boathouse window. She began to hyperventilate, dragging stuttered breaths in, and pushing little high-pitched-whines out as she pointed at the window and choked, "He's coming this way, and I think it's Spike."

"Hurry, back in the water," Grace yelled as quietly as she could, sliding back into the water with Coolcat and Loony and pulling Julia in behind her.

The boys hadn't heard her. They were still upstairs and Spike was nearly at the door. It was too late. Grace and Julia couldn't do anything but wait and watch from under the wooden floorboards and hope that Jake and Cole heard their splash and figured out something was wrong. If only they had Chippy with them, but it was too far to Chase's Lake for him to have made it here already. Julia was trying to get control of her breathing, and she was making quiet oooo, ahhh, ummm sounds when the door handle turned. Grace felt her fairy stone. It was warm. She smiled and closed her eyes.

Wait, she could see the boys. They did know. They were upstairs, crouched in a corner behind a blanket. But Cole's blonde hair was sticking out, and so was Jake's foot. Spike was pulling books from the bookshelf downstairs, looking for something.

Grace opened her eyes, "I can see them, but I have to tell them to hide better," she whispered to Julia.

Julia immediately understood. "What animal are you?"

Grace closed her eyes again. "I don't know, something small because it's up on the windowsill. Maybe a spider." She was so excited and not just because the boys were hiding. It happened again. That could only mean that she was a chosen one. She read about it last night, the Omnistone. They are only given out in extreme times and only given to a chosen sprite who will need on his or her quest to protect the waters and water animals. She had an Omnistone. She was a chosen one.

"Well do something, he's about to go up the stairs."

Grace closed her eyes again. It must be a spider because she could see that it was slowly floating down toward the floor. She watched as it quickly walked toward Jake's toes. They were huge in front of her. The spider brushed against them. Jake wiggled and pulled his toes back under the blanket. She watched again as the spider scrambled up the blanket and climbed across Cole's hair. Cole swept his hand up and shook the blanket over his head just as Spike's head rose into the room from the stairs.

Grace opened her eyes again for a second. "It's a spider and it warned them." She closed her eyes again.

Spike was rummaging through some other papers and heading for the corner where they boys were hiding, when the spider quickly dropped down onto Spike's head and scurried into his shirt pocket. Grace could see a folded piece of paper. It had lots of numbers and what looked like maybe names and addresses. The spider was nudging it up and out of the pocket. Grace couldn't see anything but the paper and the inside of the pocket. She could hear Spike moving things, then he must have bent over because the spider and the paper tumbled out onto the floor and landed just under the edge of the couch. Spike didn't even notice. And he must have found what he was looking for because by the time the spider wiggled out from under the paper, Grace could see him heading back down the stairs. She opened her eyes again.

Julia was staring wide-eyed at her. Her breathing was completely back to normal. "Are they all right?"

"Yeah, he found something and he's coming back down."

The girls heard him land on the floor above them and then he dove into the water right in front of them. He swam off into the lake. He was glowing and he didn't come up for air.

Grace and Julia quickly climbed out of the water and met Jake and Cole as they came down the stairs. Grace continued past them and headed straight up the stairs.

"Dude, that was awesome. But you should have let me take him. I might never get a chance again." Jake hit Cole in the arm, a little harder than was necessary.

"Jake, he's a criminal. You don't know what he would do if he saw us," Julia shouted. "Cole, you did the right thing."

Cole rubbed his arm. "Yeah, but Jake's right, did we just miss our opportunity?"

Grace climbed back down the stairs landing right in the middle of the group. "No, we didn't. Look at this." She held up the paper. It had names, addresses, lists of animals, and dates. "The spider took it out of his pocket."

"What is it?" Cole asked, stepping closer and reaching his hand out to take the paper.

"Oh no, you guys. Look." Julia pointed at Cole's

watch. "Time passed because we are above water. "It's already 8:15, I told my mom I would be back for breakfast at 8:15."

"But I wanted to look around more," Grace said, scanning the walls and surfaces. "And find that spider to thank him." Grace closed her eyes to see if she could still see him, but it was just black, the spider was gone, just like the eagle had gone.

"Grace, Mom will completely freak out. That means we've been underwater at camp for like five minutes. Come on." Cole pulled on his sister and jumped into the water. Grace tucked the note between the pages of her waterproof notebook, shoved it back into the Bounteous Bag, and jumped in after Cole. Jake and Julia followed right behind.

# CHAPTER 12
# JUSTICE

"Well, no one seems to have missed us," Cole said, walking out of the water and onto the shore.

"I'll meet you guys at the clubhouse after breakfast. My mom is making French toast from my cookbook." Julia smiled as her tummy rumbled. She giggled, "I guess I really am hungry this time."

"Hey, can I come?" Jake asked. "I had a raw egg shake for breakfast. I'm starving."

"Yeah, sure." Julia took Jake's hand, shaking her head, her mouth and nose pinched up at the thought of a raw egg shake. "My mom loves it when you come eat with us." She looked at Cole and Grace, "Do you want to come too?"

"Yes, please, I love French toast. Do you use maple syrup or brown sugar and butter?" Cole asked.

"Butter and cinnamon, I think." Julia replied. "But you can use whatever you want. Come on!"

*****

The kids sat around the picnic table in front of the outdoor fireplace. Grace was trying hard not to smile as she pulled out the notebook. She had to tell them. "Um guys, I know who my guide is," she blurted.

All of the kids looked at her.

"I read about it last night, but until it happened again, I couldn't believe it. I have an Omnistone. All animals are my guide," she said proudly.

"Oh that's amazing," Julia squeaked.

"Cool, Dudette. Sounds like we better keep you around," Jake laughed, punching her in the arm just a little too hard.

"That's awesome, Sis, but it seems like there's a catch," Cole said, watching his sister's face.

"It's really rare and only given to a chosen sprite and only when there is something really important that that sprite needs to do," Grace said. "I guess maybe that's now." She slipped Spike's paper out of the notebook. She spread it on the table in front of her.

"Oh," Cole said uncertainly, sitting down beside her. Julia sat on the other side and Jake was looking over her shoulder.

"What do you think this means?" Julia asked, pointing to the list.

"Well, it must be the names of the people Spike has helping him. Look, there's Walter and Fred right there. See, it even had black bear, bald eagle, and moose next to their names and the date—tomorrow," Grace said.

"Yeah, but aren't some of these older ones the things that Spike is wanted for?" Jake asked. "Remember from the library? I remember he was wanted for stealing the gorilla from that zoo in India and poaching at that safari park in Africa."

"Well, maybe he hired these guys to do the dirty work," Cole suggested, taking the list and pointing at the names. "Didn't Walter and Fred say they were being paid?"

"Yeah, but they were hired by that other guy. What did they say his name was, Julia?" Grace asked.

"I don't think he did. He just called him head honcho or something."

"Well, we don't know for sure it was Spike. He didn't seem scary today. And, he's still a water sprite, how could he hurt animals if he's a sprite?" Grace asked.

"I don't know what to think. All I know is he had something to do with my mom leaving, and I'm not any closer to finding her," Jake grumbled.

"Listen, we started this summer saying we were going to help save the animals from the oil spill, and it's been a week and we've only swam once. Look at the dates on this list. I know we saved the bear, and hopefully the eagle and moose, but there are at least twenty other animals with dates after today. I think we need to do something. I think we need to turn this list in and let the police find these people." Julia took a deep breath. "I just don't think we can do all of this ourselves. Maybe our job as sprites is to know when we need help. And, Jake, I think if we keep helping the animals we're sure to find your mom." Julia looked around at her friends.

"Yeah, I think you might be right. I mean how can we possibly do anything about this guy?" Cole asked. "He's from Brazil and it doesn't even say what he's done wrong. Spike must not have finished the list. I mean look at all of these names with nothing next to them. There's Angus

Chalfont and . . ."

"What did you just say?" Mr. Morgan demanded as he walked out of the camp. The kids were so engrossed in the conversation that they didn't even think to whisper. "What name did you just say?" Mr. Morgan repeated. His eyebrows were nearly touching and his nostrils were flared.

Cole looked up, unsure what to do. "Um, Angus Chalfont."

"Where did you hear that name?" Mr. Morgan choked out, trying to seem calm. But he was turning red and beads of sweat were beginning to form on his brow.

The kids looked at each other and Julia slowly lifted up the paper. No one stopped her. "Sorry, Dad. Those guys,

Walter and Fred, dropped it the other day." She handed the paper to her dad.

Mr. Morgan took the paper and scanned it. His eyebrows continued to creep closer and closer together. The vein running along his temple was visibly pulsing and he was gripping the paper so tight his knuckles were past turning white and were on their way to being purple. He looked up, "Don't any of you move." He turned and ran into the camp.

"I've never seen him so angry," Julia whimpered. "I'm in so much trouble." She began sobbing and heaving and having trouble breathing again. She was desperately trying to catch her breath when her mom came running out the door. She ran over to the table and sat next to Julia hugging her. "It's all right, darling. Daddy's not angry at *you*." Mrs. Morgan looked up at the kids. "That was very foolish keeping that paper. The people on that list are very dangerous people."

"How do you know?" Julia asked, sniffing and looking at her mom.

"Well, your father sometimes helps out with these things."

"But he's a civic engineer, why would he know dangerous people's names?" Julia was now sitting straight up, looking her mother in the eyes.

"Let's not worry about that right now. Right now, your father needs to get that information to the right people so that they can capture some of these terrible people."

Grace reached into her pocket to get the paper that Walter and Fred really did drop. But she remembered that Spike's name was listed on that one. Jake must have thought the same thing, because he held her arm, urging her to put the paper back in her pocket.

Mrs. Morgan smiled, "How about that French toast? Let's let Mr. Morgan worry about that piece of paper for now." Mrs. Morgan smiled again looking toward the path. "Good morning, Renee, Mark. We're so glad you were able to join us."

Grace turned and saw her parents and behind them were Jake's grandparents. Mr. Galley nodded hello and they all headed inside.

"What's happening?" Julia asked. "Why are they all so calm if those names are of criminals?"

"This is too weird. Who invited them to breakfast?" Cole asked. "Did your dad just call them and tell them?"

"I don't know," Julia sighed. "I have no idea what is going on."

"Well, I don't know who these people are, but *my* mom would be completely freaking out right now, not calmly coming here for breakfast, if she knew what just happened," Cole said. He scratched his temple and added, "What the heck is going on?"

Julia looked toward the camp. "I know. And what did my mom mean when she said my dad helps out with this *kind of thing.* How could I have missed him helping out catching dangerous criminals? What does he do, knock them over with his briefcase and drawings?" she squealed, shaking her head from side to side as tears sneaked out of her eyes yet again.

Grace looked at her friends and took a deep breath. "Do you think they all know? Know about the fairy stones, I mean? And about your mom and Spike and everything?"

"No!" Jake snapped. "They can't know about my mom. They would never lie to me about that."

"No, you're right. Sorry, Jake. I just meant that they all seem so calm, kind of like they know," Grace said.

"Well, they better not, because if they've known where my mom is all this time and not told me, I will never forgive them."

"Let's just wait and see what they say," Cole suggested as all of the adults, except for Mr. Morgan, came outside.

"Okay, kids," Mr. Galley said. "We need to talk."

"What's going on, Dad?" Cole asked.

"Just listen for now please, Cole. The list you found is a crucial piece of information. It has the names of people who committed terrible crimes against animals and the environment. I don't know how those guys came across this list, but I doubt it they were the ones who made it. The person who made it must have spent a lot of time tracking these people. Some of the names listed are new to the authorities and many of the crimes have been blamed on other people in the past. If everything on the list is true, it could mean that some of the people the government has been after may be innocent."

"Like who?" Grace asked.

Mr. Galley looked at Grace. "Well, I don't know their names, but Mr. Morgan said that this list could change things for one man in particular. If this list is true, it looks like he would be innocent of all the crimes blamed on him."

The kids looked at each other. They knew he was talking about Spike. And if Spike was innocent, then maybe they could talk to him and find Jake's mom.

"Um, do you think this innocent guy is still dangerous?" Julia asked.

Mr. Galley looked at Julia, at Grace, and then back to Julia. "Why are you asking so many questions? Do you know something more?"

"Uh, no, Dad. It's just that we happened to find out about this guy Spike today, and we think he may be the innocent one. We were kind of hoping he was a good guy," Cole said.

"It turns out Jake's mom was good friends with him. Right, Mr. and Mrs. Leftwich?" Julia added, looking at Jake's grandparents.

Jake's grandparents nodded their heads slowly.

Jake had sat silently, taking all the new information in. So, Spike may be innocent. That would make sense. Maybe his mom had been helping to make the list. Maybe his mom was working with Spike the whole time. And if Spike was here today, could it mean that maybe his mom is here too? Jake looked up. "Um, Mr. Galley, do you know what is going to happen now? I mean, like, are they going to catch those guys and clear Spike's name?"

"Well, Jake, I think so. We'll just have to wait and see. But I do know one thing, your job is to enjoy your summer, so no more talk of bad guys. Mr. Morgan will take care of them." Mr. Galley patted Jake on the back and sat down on the bench next to Cole. "Make room for me; that French toast smells delicious."

# CHAPTER 13
# FRENCH TOAST

"How about some French toast?" Mrs. Morgan asked, handing out the plates, and heading back into the camp.

Mrs. Galley smiled at the kids. "And now I have some great news." She paused for a second for the effect to sink in. "We know you've wanted to swim all week but we were thinking that after such a stressful few days, we could take you to . . . Adirondack Water World."

All four kids just stared at the adults. They had been begging to go to Adirondack Water World every year for the past, well, for as long as they could remember. And they offer it now? Today of all days?

"Jake, we know you've been wanting to check out

the surf pool and we thought today would be the perfect day," Jake's grandmother gave him a little hug.

"What do you say kids? Some French toast then a lazy river?" Mrs. Morgan asked, stepping out of the camp with a towering plate of French toast.

The kids looked at each other again. Jake's nostrils were flaring. Julia's smile stretched across her face and her knees were bouncing up and down under the table. Cole and Grace didn't know what to think. They'd be leaving first thing in the morning so they wouldn't be able to get any more information about Spike anyway.

Julia spoke first. "Yes, oh yes, please. We would love to go to the water park. Jake, it will be so cool to see you surfing in that wave pool." Julia smiled extra wide at Jake, pleading with him to give up on swimming today. "I bet the crowds will love you."

Jake couldn't help but crack half a smile. "Well, I have been dreaming about that for years."

"Yeah, and we will finally get to see you in action after all this talk over the years," Cole goaded. "And I love that toilet bowl ride. I could get flushed all day!" He laughed, thinking if he could avoid running into Pierre for another two weeks, all the better.

"Well, it sounds great to me!" Grace said. "I have the perfect bathing suit cover I can wear." And then we don't have to see Pierre, and Jake doesn't have to make any crazy decisions about following Spike, she thought to herself.

"And I have the perfect snacks to bring," Julia cheered, running over to hug Jake. "I'll even bring you something special."

Jake sunk into Julia. Maybe he should just enjoy

today. He can worry about Spike and his mom tomorrow. After all, he's waited nine years, what's one more day? "Thanks, Julia, but can it please be a store-bought snack, not a homemade one?" He rubbed his tummy. "I still can't get rid of those Cajun muffins." He lifted his bum and let out a long toot. He then began laughing like a hyena.

"Oh Jacob, that was disgusting!" his grandmother shouted.

"Sorry, Grandma, but it's not my fault. It was the muffins." Jake was laughing so hard now he was beginning to snort.

Julia stood, her mouth open and her hands on her hips. "Well I never. Jacob Leftwich you can be such a pain sometimes."

"Sorry, Jules, stressful day ya

know. Gotta have a stress reliever, right?" Jake began laughing again. "Sorry everyone. But you should try it. Woo, that felt great!" Jake began stacking his plate full of French toast, still laughing.

Cole looked at Jake with raised eyebrows, "Whatever it takes, I guess. Glad to see you happy again."

"Yeah, Jake, I'm glad you're happy again too, but maybe next time you could try one of Julia's yoga moves instead," Grace closed her eyes and began humming. "Ahhh, lalala, ummm."

Julia stomped her foot and huffed. "Grace, that's not how you do it!" She took Grace's arm and pulled her up from the picnic table. "Here, you do it like this." Julia lifted one leg and rested it against her other knee and raised both arms above her head. "See, try being a tree. Oooo, ahhh, ummm."

Jake jumped up from the table and stood in front of Julia. He leaned over, arms and legs straight making an upside down V. "Or you could be a downward dog." Jake lifted one leg and added, "Peeing on the tree."

Cole was already lying on the ground on his stomach in front of Jake. He lifted his shoulders up on straight arms and bared his teeth. "Or you could be a cobra eating the dog."

Grace lifted one leg and rested it on Julia's upraised knee. She swooped her arms into the air with her elbows bent and her hands facing out. "Or you could be a crane that lands on the tree."

Dougal and Chippy joined in.

Julia began to lose her balance and teetered slightly before falling onto Jake, who tumbled over onto Cole, who made a perfect cushion for Grace as she slowly twisted on her one leg and fell on top of the pile. They lay there laughing, forgetting about Spike and Pierre, and the job ahead of them to save the animals on the list, and to find Jake's mom. They laughed, as Dougal and Chippy jumped

on the pile and began licking at their ears and pawing at them. They were happy to just be camp kids again.

*****

That evening the camp friends returned from Adirondack Water World, exhausted and headed straight to bed.

Julia lay under her quilt giggling, remembering the pile of friends trying to do her yoga positions. But then she remembered why they were trying so hard to cheer up and nerves began creeping into her tummy, so she tried hard to replay her whole day at the water park, where not even Jake mentioned Spike, or Angus Chalfont, or his mom.

Jake hurried to bed, thanking his grandparents for an amazing day. He really did appreciate them coming to the water park. But now that he was back at camp he had other things to think about. He pulled out his mom's journals and a flashlight. Then he took a book from his bedside table about Native Americans of the Adirondacks. His dad had given him a few years ago. He would find out everything he could and then he would convince Julia to come with him to find Spike, or he would go on his own. But either way, tomorrow he had a mission.

Cole let his body sink into his bed. He hadn't realized how nervous he was about running into Pierre. This rainy week, the day at the water park, and the trip to Europe were all welcome ways of avoiding him. He had two more weeks of no Pierre.

The Eiffel Tower, the Mediterranean, Notre Dame, cobblestone streets, pastries, Grace began traveling through Europe in her mind. There was so much she wanted to see and do. She even had plans to research some of the people on Spike's list. She knew Jake would be determined to carry on the search even while they were gone, so she would have to leave him a map and maybe some suggestions. But who knows, maybe when her cousins, Carmine, Mikey, and Carolyn arrive tomorrow afternoon they could distract him with water games.

Their summer had only just begun and the water sprites were deep into new adventures.

Coming Summer 2014